To Bridie
A.M.

To Alice with love
G.W.

First published in the United States 1998 by
Little Tiger Press
N16 W23390 Stoneridge Drive, Waukesha, W1 53188
Originally published in Great Britain 1998 by
Magi Publications, London

Library of Congress Cataloging-in-Publication Data
MacDonald, Alan, 1958-
Beware of the bears! / by Alan MacDonald;
illustrated by Gwyneth Williamson.
p. cm.
Summary: Angry at what Goldilocks has done to their house,
the three bears decide to get back at her by messing up her house,
but they make an unfortunate mistake.
ISBN 1-888444-28-2
[1. Bears—Fiction. 2. Orderliness—Fiction.]
I. Williamson, Gwyneth, 1965- ill. II. Title.
PZ7.M478174Bg 1998 [E]—dc21 98-33222 CIP AC
Printed in Belgium
First American Edition
1 3 5 7 9 10 8 6 4 2

BEWARE of the BEARS!

by Alan MacDonald

illustrated by Gwyneth Williamson

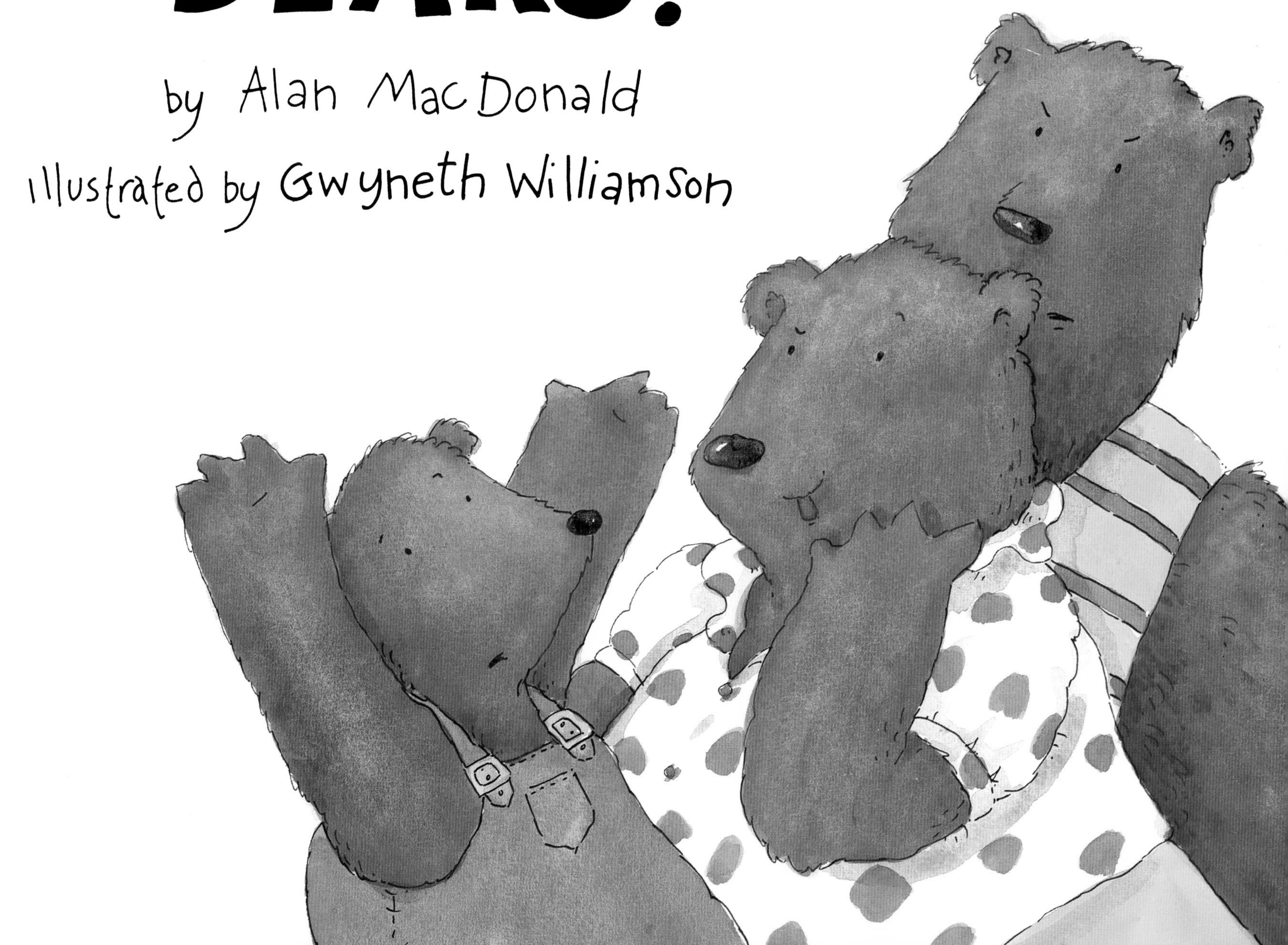

When the three bears saw what Goldilocks had done to their little cottage, they were hopping mad.

Their porridge eaten!

Chairs broken!

Beds bounced on!

"Go after her! Find out where she lives!" ordered Daddy Bear.

Baby Bear jumped
on his scooter and sped
after Goldilocks.

In no time at all he was back. "She lives on the far side of the forest," panted Baby Bear. "And what's more, she's just gone out and left her door unlocked."

"Good!" said Mommy Bear. "What are we waiting for? Let's see how *she* likes having uninvited guests."

Baby Bear led the way through the forest to Goldilocks's cottage. The door was unlocked, just as he'd said.

On the breakfast table were several open boxes. "This isn't porridge," sniffed Mommy Bear.

Baby Bear read the labels. "Wheetos, Munch Flakes, and Puffo Pops."

"Sounds all right to me," said Daddy Bear. "Pour away, Baby-o!"

“These Wheetos are too sweet,” said Daddy Bear.

“These Munch Flakes are too noisy,” said Mommy Bear.

“But these Puffo Pops are just right,” said Baby Bear, aiming a spoonful toward Daddy Bear.

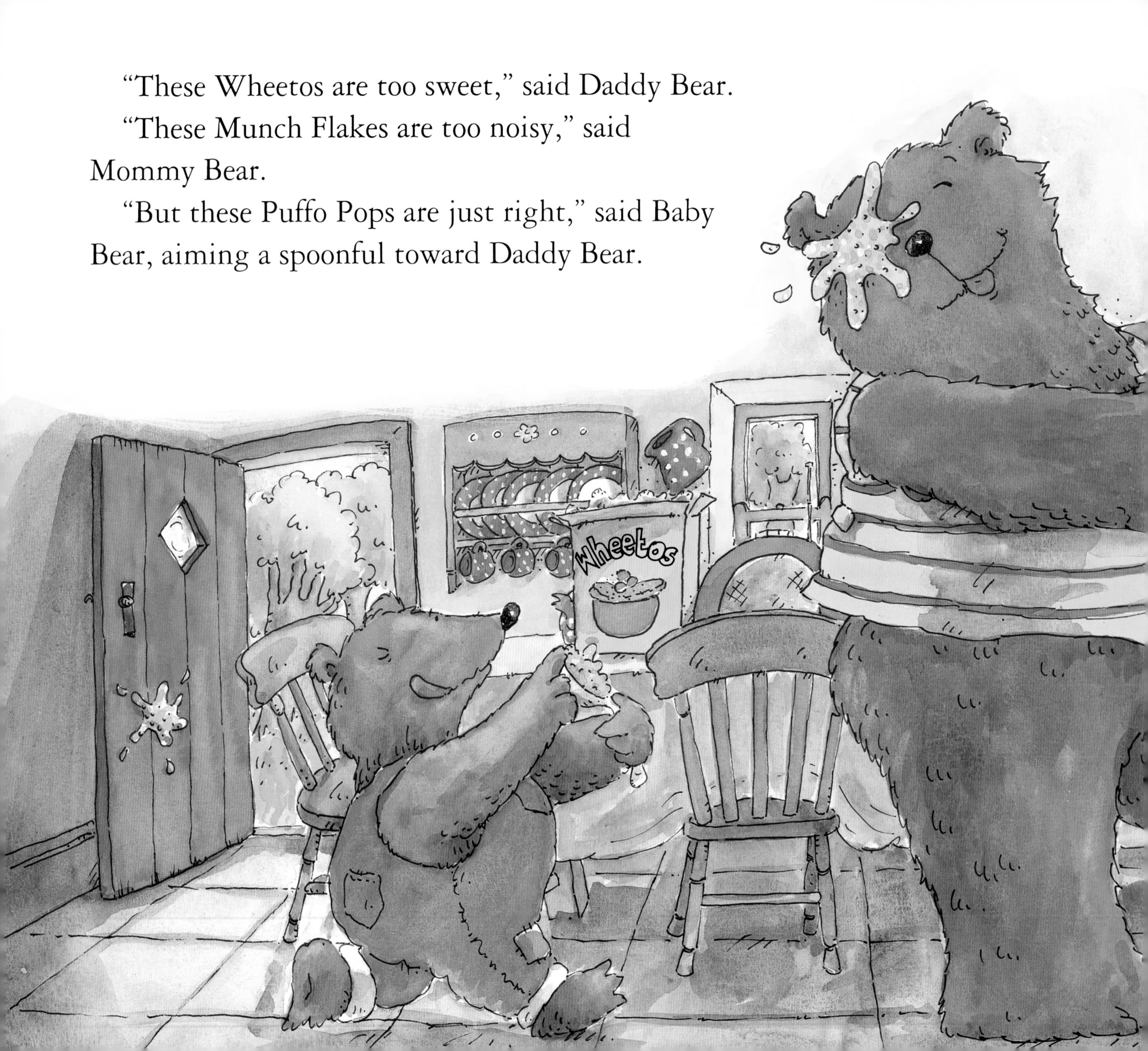

The Puffo Pops hit Daddy Bear in the eye. He launched a spoonful of Wheetos. They splattered all over Mommy Bear's best blouse.

Soon cereal was flying left and right, until the floors, the walls, and the ceiling were dripping with brown goo.

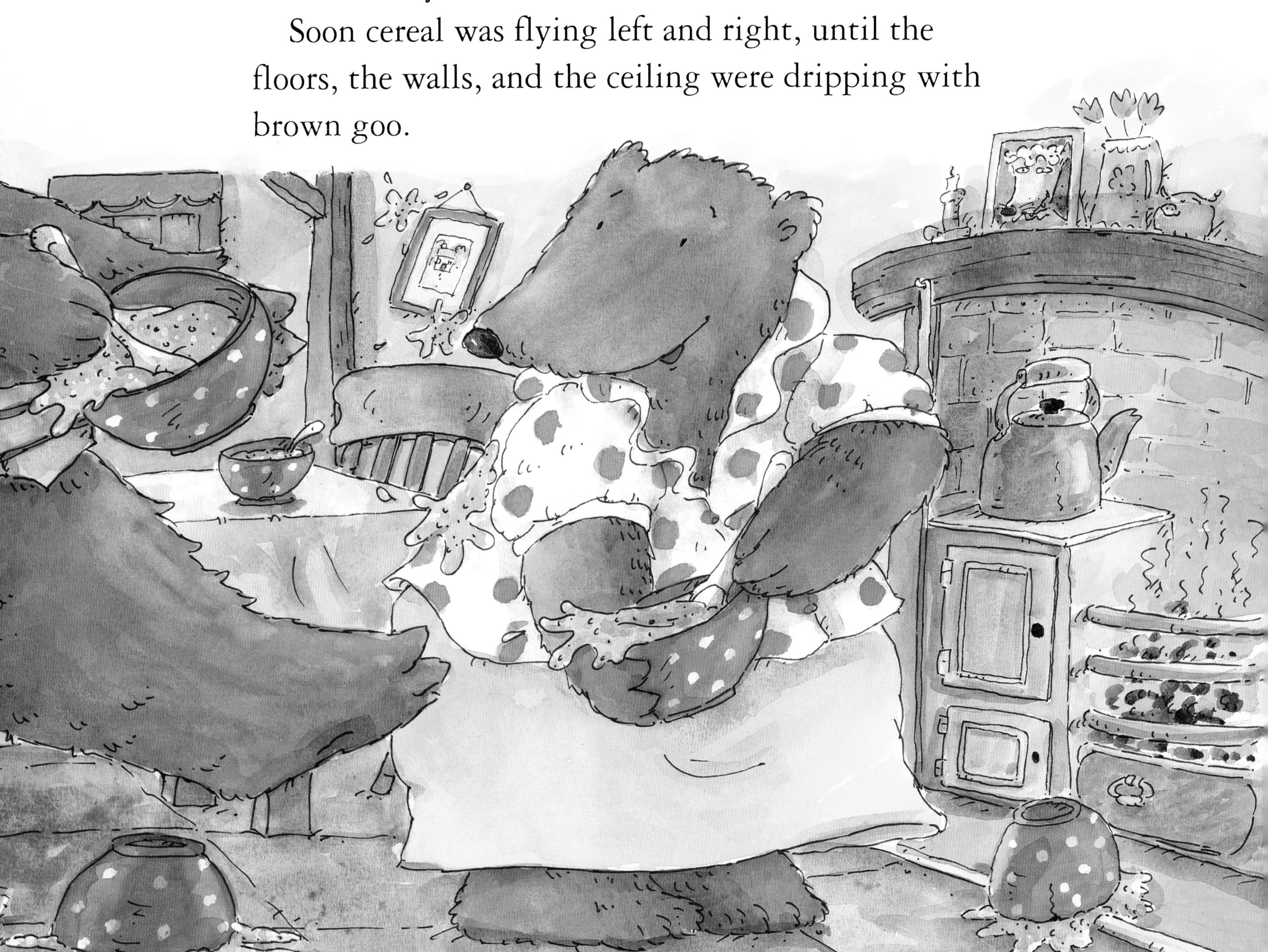

Then Baby Bear turned on the radio. “Let’s dance!” he squealed.

Mommy and Daddy Bear tangoed on the table.

“This table’s too slippy,” said Daddy Bear.

They did the cha-cha around the curtains.

"These curtains are too rippy," said Mommy Bear.

"But this sofa's just right," squeaked Baby Bear, so they all jumped on the sofa and did the bossa nova until . . .

they went right through it!

Next the three bears went upstairs. There were lots of things to try in the bathroom.

"This shaving cream's too creamy," grumbled Daddy Bear.

"This toothpaste's too minty," gargled Mommy Bear.

"But this bubble bath is just right," cried Baby Bear from beneath a mountain of suds.

"All right, here we come," said Mommy Bear.

SPLASH!

They had a wonderful
time splashing in the bath.

Once they were clean and the bathroom a mess, they moved on to the bedroom.

"These pajamas are too tight," said Daddy Bear, bursting the buttons.

"This mattress is too lumpy," said Mommy Bear, bouncing up and down.

"But these pillows are just right," said Baby Bear. "Just right for a pillow fight."

Baby Bear biffed Mommy Bear. Mommy Bear whacked Daddy Bear. Pillows split open, filling the room with clouds of feathers. Suddenly Daddy Bear stopped. “Listen!” he said. “I hear someone.”

Quietly, the three bears crept downstairs.

Goldilocks was in the kitchen. Daddy Bear, Mommy Bear, and Baby Bear gleefully spied on her from behind the door.

Goldilocks gasped when she saw the cereal splattered all over the walls.

Her eyes grew large when she saw the ripped curtains and the gigantic hole in the sofa.

She whistled when she saw the flooded bathroom decorated with shaving foam and toothpaste.

Next Goldilocks went into the bedroom. She stared openmouthed at the broken bed covered with feathers. Then the three bears jumped out from behind the door.

"Surprise!" they shouted.
"We thought *we'd* pay *you* a visit," said Mommy Bear.
Goldilocks looked at them, then back at the room . . .

and to the bears' astonishment, she threw back her head and laughed until her hair shook like golden springs.

"What's so funny?" asked Mommy Bear.

"Aren't you mad at what we've done?" added Daddy Bear.

"This isn't my house," giggled Goldilocks.

"But it must be," said Baby Bear. "I saw you go in."

"Oh, that," said Goldilocks. "The door was open, so I thought I'd look around. I'm always sneaking into other people's houses. I only came back because I left my teddy bear behind."

“Then if it’s not your house, *whose house is it?*” asked Daddy Bear.

“Oh, help!” squeaked Baby Bear, looking out of the window. . .

BEWARE of the BIG BAD WOLF!